KU-189-266

Rapunzel

First published in 2005 by
Franklin Watts
96 Leonard Street
London
EC2A 4XD

Franklin Watts Australia
45–51 Huntley Street
Alexandria
NSW 2015

Text © Hilary Robinson 2005
Illustration © Martin Impey 2005

A CIP catalogue record for this book is available
from the British Library.

ISBN 0 7496 6147 X (hbk)
ISBN 0 7496 6159 3 (pbk)

Series Editor: Jackie Hamley
Series Advisor: Dr Barrie Wade
Series Designer: Peter Scoulding

Printed in Hong Kong / China

For Andrew – H.R.

For Emilie – M.I.

Rapunzel

Retold by Hilary Robinson

Illustrated by Martin Impey

W
FRANKLIN WATTS
LONDON•SYDNEY

Once upon a time, there was a beautiful girl with long, golden hair.

Her name was Rapunzel.
A wicked witch hid her
in a tower with no door.

Rapunzel could not escape.
She was so bored that she
sang all day long.

To get into the tower the witch would cry:

Then she would climb up
Rapunzel's long hair.

One day a prince rode by.

He heard Rapunzel singing
and fell in love with her.

He watched how the witch climbed into the tower.

Later, he called:

Rapunzel, Rapunzel, let down your hair!

The Prince climbed into the tower. Rapunzel soon fell in love with him. They planned her escape.

Rapunzel made a ladder
from some silk the Prince
had brought her.

Soon she would be able
to climb out of the tower.

But when the witch next
came to see her, Rapunzel
made a big mistake.

She cried: "Why are you
so much heavier than
the Prince?"

The witch was furious.

She cut off Rapunzel's hair.

Then she hid her in
the woods.

Later, the prince rode to the tower. He called:

Rapunzel, Rapunzel, let down your hair!

But when he climbed up
he saw …

… the angry witch!
"Away!" she cried and
pushed him onto the
thorns below.

The Prince's eyes were scratched by the thorns. He couldn't see any more.

For two years he was lost in the woods.

Then, one day, he heard
beautiful singing.
"Rapunzel!" he cried.

Rapunzel's tears of joy
helped the Prince to
see again.

The Prince led Rapunzel
to his palace where they
lived happily ever after.

31

Leapfrog has been specially designed to fit the requirements of the National Literacy Strategy. It offers real books for beginning readers by top authors and illustrators.

There are 31 Leapfrog stories to choose from:

The Bossy Cockerel
Written by Margaret Nash, illustrated by Elisabeth Moseng

Bill's Baggy Trousers
Written by Susan Gates, illustrated by Anni Axworthy

Mr Spotty's Potty
Written by Hilary Robinson, illustrated by Peter Utton

Little Joe's Big Race
Written by Andy Blackford, illustrated by Tim Archbold

The Little Star
Written by Deborah Nash, illustrated by Richard Morgan

The Cheeky Monkey
Written by Anne Cassidy, illustrated by Lisa Smith

Selfish Sophie
Written by Damian Kelleher, illustrated by Georgie Birkett

Recycled!
Written by Jillian Powell, illustrated by Amanda Wood

Felix on the Move
Written by Maeve Friel, illustrated by Beccy Blake

Pippa and Poppa
Written by Anne Cassidy, illustrated by Philip Norman

Jack's Party
Written by Ann Bryant, illustrated by Claire Henley

The Best Snowman
Written by Margaret Nash, illustrated by Jörg Saupe

Eight Enormous Elephants
Written by Penny Dolan, illustrated by Leo Broadley

Mary and the Fairy
Written by Penny Dolan, illustrated by Deborah Allwright

The Crying Princess
Written by Anne Cassidy, illustrated by Colin Paine

Jasper and Jess
Written by Anne Cassidy, illustrated by François Hall

The Lazy Scarecrow
Written by Jillian Powell, illustrated by Jayne Coughlin

The Naughty Puppy
Written by Jillian Powell, illustrated by Summer Durantz

Freddie's Fears
Written by Hilary Robinson, illustrated by Ross Collins

Cinderella
Written by Barrie Wade, illustrated by Julie Monks

The Three Little Pigs
Written by Maggie Moore, illustrated by Rob Hefferan

Jack and the Beanstalk
Written by Maggie Moore, illustrated by Steve Cox

The Three Billy Goats Gruff
Written by Barrie Wade, illustrated by Nicola Evans

Goldilocks and the Three Bears
Written by Barrie Wade, illustrated by Kristina Stephenson

Little Red Riding Hood
Written by Maggie Moore, illustrated by Paula Knight

Rapunzel
Written by Hilary Robinson, illustrated by Martin Impey

Snow White
Written by Anne Cassidy, illustrated by Melanie Sharp

The Emperor's New Clothes
Written by Karen Wallace, illustrated by François Hall

The Pied Piper of Hamelin
Written by Anne Adeney, illustrated by Jan Lewis

Hansel and Gretel
Written by Penny Dolan, illustrated by Graham Philpot

The Sleeping Beauty
Written by Margaret Nash, illustrated by Barbara Vagnozzi